HELLO KITTY
and friends

The Friendship Club

HarperCollins *Children's Books*

MEET HELLO KITTY
and friends

Hello Kitty

Mimmy

Tammy

Mama

Papa

Grandpa

Grandma

Fifi

Dear Daniel

With special thanks to
Linda Chapman and Michelle Misra

First published in Great Britain by HarperCollins *Children's Books* in 2013

www.harpercollins.co.uk
1 3 5 7 9 10 8 6 4 2
ISBN: 978-000-751433-5

Printed and bound in England by Clays Ltd, St Ives plc.

MIX
Paper from
responsible sources
FSC™ C007454

FSC™ is a non-profit international organisation established to promote
the responsible management of the world's forests. Products carrying the
FSC label are independently certified to assure consumers that they come
from forests that are managed to meet the social, economic and
ecological needs of present and future generations,
and other controlled sources.

Find out more about HarperCollins and the environment at
www.harpercollins.co.uk/green

Contents

1. The First Day.................................9

2. Making Friends.............................19

3. Hello Kitty's Friendship Club....41

4. The First Meeting.......................53

5. Telling the Truth.......................70

6. Hello Kitty's Super Idea............83

The First Day

Hello Kitty checked the mirror on her dressing table. The red bow in her hair still didn't look quite right. She pushed it up a little. Today was the first day of her new school and she wanted to look perfect.

Hello Kitty's tummy felt quivery with excitement. A new school meant a new teacher and making new friends. How exciting was that?

She inspected her reflection. She was wearing a checked pinafore dress, and a white blouse with puff sleeves and the most perfect little buttons that shone like *diamonds*. She liked her new uniform. At her old school, they all had to wear exactly the same uniform but at this new school it was completely different. As long as you wore the school colours and looked neat and tidy, you could wear whatever dress, top, skirt or trousers you liked. Hello Kitty had had great

fun shopping with her twin sister, Mimmy, and

their Mama.

Hello Kitty did a little twirl and her skirt

spun out. There was still one

thing missing though. Lip

balm! She picked up a pot

of Strawberry Surprise

and rubbed a little on to

her lips to make them soft

and slightly shiny. That was it. She was now

officially ***ready!***

Mama's voice called up the stairs — it was

time to go.

Super! Picking up her bright red spotty

rucksack, Hello Kitty ran out of her bedroom.

Mimmy was standing with Mama and Papa

at the bottom of the staircase. Mimmy's school

uniform was much simpler than Hello Kitty's –

a red pinafore and a neat white polo shirt – and

her yellow bow was on the right of her head,

not the left. They always wore their bows on different sides so people could tell them apart.

Papa had on his smart work suit for his job in the city, and was ready to take them both to school – he would drop them off that morning, and Mama would collect them later.

Papa tweaked their noses and kissed Mama on the cheek.

Mama smiled at him and both the girls, and they all hugged tightly. A new school would be so **exciting!** And as a special treat, they would have Mama's famous Apple Pie for tea that night. Yummy! It was the girls' favourite.

Hello Kitty and Mimmy got in to the back seat of the car and Mama waved them off as they drove away with Papa.

Mimmy was clutching her yellow school bag, and looked a bit nervous. She was much shyer than Hello Kitty, and was worried about making new friends.

But at least Alice would be in her class. Alice was Mimmy's friend from before. Hello Kitty also had one old friend in her class. His name was Dear Daniel.

Hello Kitty and Dear Daniel had been friends since they were very little, although up until now they had always gone to different schools. They hadn't seen each other much as Dear Daniel was often away travelling because his dad was a photographer. But he and Hello Kitty always wrote to each other. Now he would be in her class. **Hooray!**

POST CARD

Dear Hello Kitty,

Having a great time
on safari!
Wish you were here!

Love,
Dear Daniel
X

Hello Kitty

London

Mimmy explained that she was worried in case she didn't make any friends but Papa reassured her that she'd be fine. He was sure she'd make friends in one of the clubs they had at lunchtime or after school. Perhaps Mimmy could join a music club! Mimmy loved music.

Hello Kitty wondered what clubs SHE would join. She liked all sorts of things – designing clothes, art and craft, baking, dancing. Most of all, though, she liked making friends. That was definitely the best thing in the **whole wide world!** Though she wasn't sure there would be a club for that!

She watched the streets of London as they whizzed by – the buses, the taxis, the people and cars. Her stomach felt as if it was filled with popping candy. Oh, what was their first day going to be like?

Making Friends

Hello Kitty stood with Mimmy and Papa
and looked through the school gates. The
playground was full of children. They were all
running round and calling out to each other.
The school was **so big** – **much bigger**

than her old school.

They all looked around at the crowds of people, then Mimmy spotted someone she knew. Alice! She ran over to her friend to say hello.

Hello Kitty started to follow them but then she saw a girl whose mum was just leaving. Hello Kitty paused. The girl had dark brown hair and her uniform was very neat and tidy – a white shirt and yellow knee-length dress. Could this girl become her first friend at the new school? Hello Kitty smiled at her.

The girl smiled back. But just then she

dropped her school bag. It fell to the ground,

spilling books and pencils **everywhere!**

Throwing her hands in the air in dismay, the

girl quickly started picking everything up.

Hello Kitty ran over to help, and the girl

smiled her thanks.

They chatted happily as Hello Kitty helped her pick up her things. The girl's name was Tammy, and she had a twin brother, Timmy. He was going to be in Class 3B, but Tammy was in Class 3A – the same as Hello Kitty!

Hello Kitty was thrilled. Mimmy was going to be in class 3B too, and Hello Kitty was just about to tell Tammy all about her twin, when she thought she heard someone call her name…

Hello Kitty swung round to look. Dear Daniel! He had a big grin on his face.

She called out in delight, and clapped her hands.

Hello Kitty introduced Dear Daniel to Tammy. He would be in the same class as them both – how super was that!

Dear Daniel **smiled**, his eyes crinkling up. He scooped up Tammy's remaining things, and handed them to her. Tammy had lots of books with her!

Tammy loved reading. It was one of her favourite things.

Dear Daniel did too, but he especially loved books about animals. But Tammy liked books about everything!

Hello Kitty thought reading was brilliant too, but she also loved other things like baking and drawing and painting and dancing and fashion.

She smiled at them both, and they smiled back at her. Hello Kitty was so happy she wanted to *jump* for joy. It looked like she had some friends at her new school already!

She linked arms with them both. This was going to be fun – now that they had each other!

Hello Kitty turned to wave goodbye to Papa and then it was time to go inside. Class 3A's teacher was called Miss Davey. She had dark glossy hair, big eyes and very red lipstick. She was wearing a stylish red skirt and black blouse.

She smiled at her class, and waved
them all in to take their seats.

The tables were arranged so
that either four or six people could sit together
so Hello Kitty, Dear Daniel and Tammy sat
down at a table for four. Hello Kitty got
her pencil case out and started to arrange
everything neatly on the table. She had spent
ages with Mimmy choosing their
new school things. They both
had a rubber in the shape
of a watermelon slice, two
pencils which were pink
with white dots, a silver pen

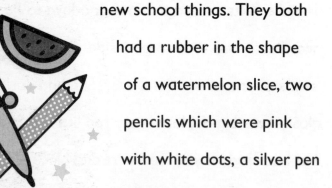

and a new pencil sharpener in the shape of a

pink **sparkly** bow.

Miss Davey called for quiet and started to

take the register. She had almost finished when

the door burst open and a girl came running in.

Her hair was escaping from her ponytail and

her shirt was flapping over the top of her skirt.

She had a flower in her hair and one sock

was pulled up, the other

rolled down. Her bag

was decorated with

swirls of paint.

She was almost late,

but had made it into

class just in time for her name to be called from the register! Her name was Fifi.

The girl bounced into her seat, and her curls bounced up and down just like she did.

She sat next to Hello Kitty. Her eyes were sparkling, and she was slightly out of breath.

She chattered away – she had been at ice-skating practice and then got stuck in traffic on the way to school, and then…

Miss Davey looked over, her eyebrows raising.

Miss Davey looked away and Fifi turned to smile at Hello Kitty. Hello Kitty smiled back, liking her already. Ice-skating before school. How **exciting** was that!

Hello Kitty turned back to listen to Miss Davey. They had to copy down their weekly timetable from the whiteboard. Whilst they did that, Miss Davey told them a little bit about herself — how she lived in a small house by the park. She had no children but she had a dog called Spot. Hello Kitty liked the sound of that.

Fifi made a few quick **drawings** on the bottom of her exercise book and then nudged Hello Kitty. Hello Kitty looked down. Fifi had drawn two dogs. There was a little poodle with its hair in waves, and a spaniel with huge eyes. Beside it Fifi had written, 'which type of dog do you think Spot is?'

The drawings were brilliant.

Miss Davey looked over at them huddled together, then came over and held out her hand for the drawing.

Oh no! Hello Kitty didn't want to get into

trouble. But Miss Davey had reached over and

picked up the exercise book.

Hello Kitty and Fifi held their breath as Miss Davey studied the drawings. And then, to Hello Kitty's relief, Miss Davey started to chuckle. They weren't in trouble at all! Miss Davey said she was pleased to have such a talented artist in the class and she was looking forward to seeing more of Fifi's drawings.

Phew! Hello Kitty breathed out, and she and Fifi picked up their pens again.

Miss Davey turned back to the whiteboard and put up a picture of a scruffy black and white dog. She wrote **'SPOT'** underneath in big letters, and turned back to Fifi. Maybe Fifi could do a drawing of what Spot actually looked like, just for Miss Davey?

Fifi beamed at her, and winked at Hello Kitty. Of course she could!

By break time, Hello Kitty was having so much fun. Dear Daniel was as lovely as he always was. Tammy and Fifi had so much

energy. They were the perfect four! Hello Kitty

was very pleased they were all sitting at the

same table, although the other people in her

class seemed like fun too.

When the bell rang for break they all took their snacks outside. Tammy's twin brother ran over to say hello but then headed off to play football with some other boys. Mimmy was playing with Alice and a couple of new friends. She looked very **happy**. Hello Kitty found herself looking forward to going home time – it was going to be great to share the news about their day!

Hello Kitty looked at her new friends. What did they think they should do now? She had lots of ideas.

Dear Daniel, Fifi and Tammy all shrugged. It looked like it would be up to Hello Kitty to decide what to do, which was perfect. She was great at thinking of things.

Hello Kitty smiled, and pulled out her notepad. Hmmm… They could decide what clubs they were going to join! There was

♫ **Music Club**,

Drama Club, ♪

Art Club…

Fifi squealed when Hello Kitty said Art Club – she'd love to join that one!

Hello Kitty and Tammy nodded and said they would join too, but Dear Daniel wasn't sure – he preferred outdoor things to art.

Hello Kitty looked at the list.

Tammy looked over her shoulder. Perhaps

they could all join another one together?

There was Science Club, Gardening Club…

Dear Daniel would definitely join that one!

Tammy said she would too, but Fifi shook her head. Oh dear.

Hello Kitty sighed. It would be nice if they could all do one club together. There must be something they all liked. She carried on reading out the list but there wasn't any one club they all wanted to join.

Fifi laughed. It looked like they would just have to do different things!

Unless, someone could invent their very own **special** club so they could all be in the same one...

That was it! Hello Kitty gasped. Fifi's words had just made her think of the most wonderful idea. They would have their own club, not just for school, but for all of the time, every day.

Dear Daniel wrinkled up his brow. It was a brilliant idea, but what could they call it?

Hello Kitty's eyes shone. She'd had another

brilliant idea about that - they would call it

★ ★ **The Friendship Club** ★ ★

of course!

Hello Kitty's Friendship Club

The Friendship Club! Fifi jumped up and down in glee. It was perfect!

Tammy and Dear Daniel also loved the idea of the Friendship Club. Hello Kitty's mind was soon racing with plans. They would have meetings and membership cards and a password! All sorts of things!

Tammy was curious though. What did you do in a Friendship Club?

But that was what was so great about it. They could decide the things they all liked to do, and do them! Things like baking and shopping and having sleepovers... Hello Kitty started scribbling her favourite things in her notepad.

Fifi was very excited. She loved sleepovers!

Hello Kitty started listing things they could do - from organising parties and having fashion

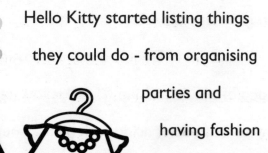

days, to clothes swaps and painting their nails...
She wrote them all down as fast as she could.

But Dear Daniel interrupted. He wasn't very
keen on the idea of painting his nails!

Hello Kitty giggled, and agreed. But they did
need to have a meeting and decide on the rules
of the club.

The others nodded eagerly.

Hello Kitty thought hard. Maybe she could ask Mama if everyone could come to her house tomorrow after school? They could all come round for tea. It would be lots of fun.

The group of friends all looked at each other excitedly. This was going to be **great!**

Once Hello Kitty got home she asked Mama if her friends could come round. Mama said yes, of course, so Hello Kitty sat down at her dressing table and started making a list of all the things she wanted to get ready before the

very first meeting of The Friendship Club:

1. Make membership cards

2. Get paper out to write down rules

3. Think of some games to play

4. Make special Friendship Club cupcakes for everyone...

Hello Kitty chewed the end of her pencil. What else? She wanted everyone to have a great time and for it to be the *best club ever*. Suddenly she had another idea – maybe she could ask Mama if she could have some

spare ribbon from the sewing cupboard so

she could make all of the girls matching

Friendship Club bows to wear in their

hair. But what about Dear Daniel?

Of course! He could have

Friendship Club shoelaces instead.

Perfect! There was so much to do – she'd

better get started!

Hello Kitty had made cupcakes lots of

times before, so she didn't even need to look at

the recipe. She measured the flour and sugar

and eggs and whisked everything up before

spooning the mixture into pretty cupcake cases.

Then she got Mama to help her put them in the oven. She licked the spoon and cleared everything away before sitting down at the table to make the Friendship Club membership cards. She decorated each one with an identical border of hearts and wrote on each of them in a sparkly pen:

HELLO KITTY
Friendship Club

Name.............................
Address.........................
Birthday.........................
Likes.............................
Dislikes.........................

HEL...
Fri...

Name.............................
Address.........................
Birthday.........................
Likes.............................
Dislikes.........................

Then she found a large piece of paper and wrote 'FRIENDSHIP CLUB RULES' in different coloured letters at the top, and after that she wrote a list of games they could play at the first meeting.

Meanwhile, Mama had put the cakes to cool on a wire rack. Hello Kitty decorated them with **white icing**

and sugar hearts. She made sure each one was identical so that every member of the club would have a cake that was exactly the same.

She had been so busy getting everything

ready! Mama gave her a hug as Hello Kitty

finished the cakes and sat down with the ribbon.

The Friendship Club was going to be super-well

organised.

Mimmy was walking past, and looked

curiously at the membership

cards and cakes on the

table. Quickly, Hello

Kitty explained what

the club was all about.

Maybe Mimmy and

Alice could join too?

Mimmy gave Hello Kitty a hug. It was a

l♥vely idea, but she thought she and

Alice were going to be too busy with Music

Club and things to join another club.

But Hello Kitty didn't mind – she'd still see

Mimmy all the time, at home and at school!

The two sisters smiled at each other, and Hello Kitty felt a warm rush of happiness. She couldn't wait for the Friendship Club's first meeting!

The First Meeting

Everything was ready! Hello Kitty, Fifi,

Tammy and Dear Daniel met up the next

morning in the playground at school. The

meeting was going to be totally... **super!**

Everyone liked the sound of that. Dear Daniel

grinned at Hello Kitty, and she smiled back.

Today felt very super!

Hello Kitty got more and more excited all day. By going-home-time, she could hardly sit still. She and Fifi almost fell off their chairs with excitement. Miss Davey came over to their

table, wondering what was going on. Why were they all so energetic?

Fifi giggled.

Hello Kitty tried to sit still, and explained to Miss Davey about how they were all going back to her house after school. It was going to be **so much fun!**

Miss Davey shook her head at them all as the bell went, and waved them out of the classroom with a big grin on her face.

The four of them fetched their bags and then went out to the playground where Mama was waiting.

Mimmy was going to Alice's house for tea. She called out to Hello Kitty, and waved goodbye to her.

Mama got her car keys out. It was time to go!

Hello Kitty had set everything out. They all sat down and she gave out the membership cards. Everyone's card was just the same. Hello Kitty explained that they needed to fill in the details of their own cards, and she handed round some pens. And while they were filling them in — they could eat their Friendship Club cupcakes! She took the lid off the tin.

Everyone made hungry noises when they saw the **beautiful** cupcakes Hello Kitty had made. Dear Daniel was amazed; they were all exactly the same! They must have taken ages to make.

Hello Kitty explained that in proper clubs everyone had the same things. She showed them all the bows she had made for everyone too. They would be able to wear them on the left side of their heads to show they were part of the Friendship Club! And Dear Daniel had shoelaces, not a bow, so he would have something to wear too.

Hello Kitty handed them out, and thought about what they still needed to do. Hmmm… They needed to make up a password, and decide things everyone in the club liked and didn't like. And think of what they should do next!

A password was simple - everyone voted for *Super!* Hello Kitty beamed. That had been easy!

That meant it was time to write down some Friendship Club rules. She picked up the pen, and found a big sheet of paper they could use.

Number one: the Friendship Club should always wear their bow or shoelaces to meetings and the bow should always be worn on the left side.

Fifi looked a bit unsure about this idea. They didn't need too many rules, did they?

Hello Kitty wrote the first rule down on the big sheet of paper, and smiled at Fifi to reassure her. They would only need a few rules, just enough to make it a proper club. She turned back to the piece of paper. Rule number two: Friendship Club members should have their membership card with them at all times. **And for rule number three, she wrote:** Friendship Club members should always try and *be* stylish! **She looked round happily and saw that Tammy and Dear Daniel were looking worried.**

Tammy and Dear Daniel looked down at what they were wearing, then back at Hello Kitty. Neither of them thought they were very good at being stylish!

Hello Kitty giggled. They were already stylish, but it would be OK, she'd help them too! And now that they had some rules, they could decide on their favourite Friendship Club things. They would start with a favourite colour. Could it be pink? Hello Kitty loved pink!

But Tammy liked blue.

And Fifi liked purple.

And Dear Daniel liked red.

Oh no! What could they possibly do?

Tammy looked round nervously at Fifi and Dear Daniel. Pink would be fine as a favourite colour, wouldn't it?

They all nodded.

Hello Kitty smiled and wrote The Friendship Club's favourite colour is pink. She looked up at her friends. What was their favourite trip out going to be?

Fifi suggested ice-skating.
Tammy wanted it to
be going dancing.
And Dear Daniel liked

going to the park!

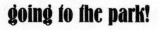

Fifi thought ice-skating was

more fun than both of those.

But Tammy didn't know how

to ice-skate, and Dear Daniel

would still prefer to go to the park.

Hello Kitty thought hard. How were they

ever going to agree? What if they thought

about what their favourite thing was to do

inside instead? There were so many things - it

could be baking, fashion makeovers…

But Fifi wanted it to be drawing.

Tammy said tentatively that maybe it could be painting?

Dear Daniel came up with model-making.

And Hello Kitty thought maybe it could be reading!

Oh dear, they simply couldn't agree. The meeting wasn't going as Hello Kitty had imagined AT ALL. She had wanted everyone to have fun. She quickly suggested that it might be a good idea to decide on their favourite things later – maybe they could play a game instead? What about Hide and Seek?

Everyone nodded eagerly. They all loved to

play Hide and Seek!

Phew! That was a relief.

They were soon having a great time playing. Afterwards, Tammy told them stories. She was very good at making them up.

When she had finished they got some paper out and all drew the characters from the stories. By the time everyone's parents arrived they had forgotten they hadn't been able to agree on the rules and were laughing and talking.

Hello Kitty reminded her friends to remember the secret password, and to wear their bows and shoelaces to school the next day, as she waved them all off.

Mama put an arm around her shoulder, and asked her how the first meeting had gone.

For a moment Hello Kitty remembered how they hadn't been able to agree, but then she thought about the games they had played and how much fun they'd had. It had been *Super!*

Mama was really pleased, and smiled at Hello Kitty. Her eyes shone as she mentioned that there might be a little piece of her Apple Pie left over from the night before, and did Hello Kitty

think she maybe had room for a slice?

Hello Kitty grinned happily – of course

she did!

Telling the Truth

Hello Kitty ran ahead of Mimmy into school the next day. She couldn't wait to see her friends. They would all be wearing their bows and Dear Daniel would be wearing his shoelaces!

She stopped as she went through the gates.

Fifi was wearing her bow just like Hello Kitty,

but Tammy's bow was in the middle and Dear

Daniel wasn't wearing his special shoelaces at

all! **Oh no!**

Hello Kitty hurried over to remind him that he should be wearing them, and she called out to him.

Dear Daniel looked at his feet. Hello Kitty listened as he explained that he didn't really forget them. He thought they were **great**, but boys didn't really wear coloured shoelaces to school, so he thought he'd just wear them to the Friendship Club meetings.

Tammy was wearing her bow but it was in the middle. Hadn't they been going to wear them on the left?

Tammy looked a bit sheepish, but said she definitely preferred to wear her bow in the middle. Hello Kitty thought about this, and let out a little sigh. Wasn't trying to be the same and doing the same things what being in a club was all about?

Tammy and Fifi looked at Hello Kitty awkwardly. Fifi said that she didn't really want to be the same as everyone else. She said that she was sorry, and still wanted to be friends, but just not part of the club. Fifi turned and walked away.

Hello Kitty stared. **What was happening?**

Tammy asked her if she was OK.

Hello Kitty swallowed. Did everyone agree with Fifi? Should everything be different in their club? Maybe if Fifi didn't want to be in it, there shouldn't be a club at all. Hello Kitty was so confused.

Tammy still wanted to be in the club, but Dear

Daniel wasn't as sure. He still wanted to be friends, but the club just didn't seem to be about the things he liked doing. He hoped Hello Kitty would understand.

Hello Kitty nodded quietly, but she wasn't very happy, and kept her head down.

Just then the bell rang and they all had to get into line. Hello Kitty had wanted the Friendship Club to be so much fun for everyone. **Whatever could she do?**

Hello Kitty couldn't concentrate on her work that morning. All she could think about was how the Friendship Club wasn't working out

at all! As the bell went for break, she hurried

outside. Mimmy was sitting on the bench

with Alice.

Mimmy saw her face and knew something was wrong straightaway. She asked Hello Kitty what the matter was, and Hello Kitty found the whole story bursting out of her. She told Mimmy all about what had happened, about her friends and how they didn't want to be in the Friendship Club any more.

Mimmy **hugged** her tightly.

Hello Kitty was so unhappy. She had just wanted the Friendship Club to be fun, and for them all to be the same. That was what being in a club was all about, wasn't it?

But Mimmy and Alice weren't so sure. Why did friends have to be the same? Friends could be different in lots of ways. Mimmy loved playing the flute and the piano, and Alice loved playing the violin. It didn't stop them being friends.

Hello Kitty listened to them, and played with her buttons. She hadn't thought about it like that. She'd just thought about being in a club.

She kept listening as Mimmy explained that it was really good to be different. Alice went to gymnastic classes, so she was able to teach her how to do a *cartwheel*, and Mimmy taught Alice how to bake cupcakes because she loved cooking. The more Hello Kitty thought about it, the more it became clear that it might not be as much fun to be exactly the same as all

your friends. It was like their new uniform. It was nice to be the same but also to be a bit different from everyone else.

Hello Kitty was thinking hard now. Perhaps Mimmy and Alice were right! She *liked* the fact that she was able to wear a uniform that was slightly different from everyone else's. But what if she'd messed everything up with her friends for good?

Hello Kitty glanced over to where Fifi, Tammy and Dear Daniel were standing just a little way away. Maybe they still wanted to be

friends with her? She knew Mimmy was right, but she was still sad that they didn't want to be part of the Friendship Club.

Unless… Suddenly one of her **special**, **super**, Hello Kitty bright ideas suddenly popped into her head. Her eyes widened, and she looked at her sister. Hello Kitty knew just what she needed to do!

Hello Kitty's Super Idea

Fifi came over to where Hello Kitty was

sitting. She was very sorry she had said she

didn't want to be in the Friendship Club. But

Hello Kitty wasn't upset any more. She jumped

to her feet and smiled at Fifi, her idea racing

through her head.

The most important

thing was definitely

that they could all

still be friends!

Fifi blinked at her, surprised. She had always

wanted to be Hello Kitty's friend! Dear Daniel

and Tammy came over too. Hello Kitty didn't

want to give too much away – but asked if they

could all come to her house at six o'clock that

evening?

Everyone was sure they could, but what was

going on? Hello Kitty grinned. They'd just have

to wait and see!

Luckily Mama agreed to everyone coming round. She didn't know what was going on, but looking at Hello Kitty's determined face, she could tell it was something important.

Hello Kitty set to work cutting, **drawing**, pasting, baking. She finished just in time to run upstairs, brush her hair and put some lip balm on and then she was ready. The doorbell rang and her friends arrived, still wondering why they were there. Tammy gave an excited laugh.

Hello Kitty led them into the room, and they all stopped and gasped. On one wall was a long banner with the words:

THE FRIENDSHIP CLUB!

on it. Beneath it, Hello Kitty had drawn her friends, each doing something they liked – Fifi was ice skating, Tammy was reading a book, Dear Daniel was making a model and Hello Kitty herself was baking.

She pointed them all to their seats.

On each place at the table there was a brand new membership card. Dear Daniel looked at his – it had animals drawn on it!

Fifi had ice skates and paints on hers, and Tammy's had books and music. They all had different cards. It was cool!

In fact, it was better than cool – it was **super!**

Hello Kitty opened the tin of cupcakes. There was one for everyone – Dear Daniel's had red icing, Fifi's had purple, Tammy's had blue and

Hello Kitty's had pink. Hello Kitty explained her idea to her friends. They should have a new Friendship Club. One without rules!

She grinned as she saw her friends' faces. Everyone could be as different as they wanted. They could **SHARE** their favourite things. Dear Daniel could take them to the park and show them fun things to do there and Tammy could take them dancing. Hello Kitty would be able to show all of them her favourite shops, and Fifi could take them ice-skating!

Her friends were all amazed. Tammy looked

round – she could hardly believe that Hello

Kitty had done all of this for them! The banner,

the cards, the cakes…

Dear Daniel smiled. He could believe it; he'd

known Hello Kitty the longest, and knew that

she was the best friend

anyone could ever have!

Hello Kitty saw

how pleased all her

friends were, and

blushed. Fifi put

her arm around

her, and pulled her

into a hug.

A Friendship Club hug! The others joined in and they all hugged tightly.

Hello Kitty looked at her friends hopefully. She was sure they'd all want to be members of the new Friendship Club. The new, *different* Friendship Club.

Everyone smiled at each other as though to confirm it and they all began to chatter excitedly at once. Now that they had their club again, what should they do next? Should they play Hide and Seek again?

But Fifi stopped them. She thought they **did** need some rules for the Friendship Club.

Hello Kitty blinked. Rules? What was going on?

Fifi explained what she meant. Not rules like they had before, but just rules about what being a good friend was all about. Fifi took up a new big piece of paper and wrote 'The Friendship Club Rules' at the top. She looked up at her

friends. What could the first rule be? Hmmm.
Something about it being OK for good friends
to be different from each other?

Hello Kitty gave a small cry and her eyes
sparkled. Fifi gave her the pen and Hello Kitty
wrote in big letters:

Good Friends
come in
all shapes
and sizes

They all cheered.

It was perfect! They had their first

Friendship Club rule.

Hello Kitty grinned. She knew it wouldn't

be the last rule, but for now… She paused and

looked at the others.

Now, it was time for some seriously super

FUN!

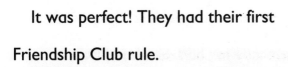

They had a **great** time playing. After

everyone had gone home, Hello Kitty cleared

up and got ready for bed. She had just put

her nightie on – it was pink with big red

strawberries printed on it – when the door

opened and Mimmy came in to see how

everything had gone. She sat down on Hello

Kitty's bed. The twins each had their own

bedroom although they often slept in each

other's rooms.

Hello Kitty happily told her all about it – how everyone had loved the new Friendship Club, and how everything was just brilliant now, and how she couldn't have done it without Mimmy's help. She went over and sat down beside her, and Mimmy gave her a big hug.

Hello Kitty hugged her back. She looked at her sister. Even though she had the Friendship Club, Mimmy would always be her very best friend.

And Hello Kitty would be Mimmy's! For always and ever.

Hello Kitty and Mimmy smiled at each other, and then Mimmy went off to her own room to go to sleep. Hello Kitty sat back on her bed, her thoughts starting to whirl with plans of all the things she could do with her friends… sleepovers, trips out, making things, organising things.

Oh yes, they were going to have fun - lots of it! **SUPER!**

Turn over the page for activities and
fun things that you can do with your
friends – just like Hello Kitty!

Make your own Friendship Club Membership Card!

Follow the instructions and suggestions to make your own card, so you can join Hello Kitty and Friends in their club too.

ALWAYS ASK A GROWN-UP FOR HELP BEFORE USING SCISSORS! ★ ★ ★

You will need:

- Glue
- Scissors
- Tracing paper
- Paper and cardboard
- A photo of yourself
- Coloured pencils to decorate your card

1. Trace, photocopy or cut out the membership card template on page 103. You can also print a template out at **www.harpercollins.co.uk/ HelloKittyandFriends**

2. Stick the template on to some cardboard and cut it to size

3. Cut out and glue your photo into the space provided

4. Fill in your details

Why not make your membership card even more special?

Colour your card different colours – the brighter the better! Cut out pictures of things you like to do from magazines, and stick them on.

Glue on some glitter or sequins to really make your card sparkle!

Make membership cards for some of your friends! Go to **www.harpercollins.co.uk/ HelloKittyandFriends** to print out more templates if you need them.

HELLO KITTY
Friendship Club

Name..

Birthday...

Likes...

Dislikes..

My Best Friend is............................

Stick your
photo here

Trace, cut out or
photocopy the
template. Always ask
a grown-up for help
before using scissors!

HELLO KITTY
Friendship Club

Are you starting at a new school, just like *Hello Kitty?*
Check out these ideas for making your notebooks and pens even more stylish!

ALWAYS ASK A GROWN-UP FOR HELP BEFORE USING SCISSORS!

Save the wrapping paper from special presents and use it to cover and decorate your books. Patterns, bows and ribbons are all perfect – gorgeous!

Glue the end of a long pretty ribbon to your pen, near the top. Wrap it all the way around to cover it, before gluing the end down too. Finish by gluing on a bow of the same ribbon. Super!

Hello Kitty loves making her stationery sparkle. It means it's one of a kind – just like her.

105

Dip the round eraser on the end of a pencil in some paint, and press it to make a spot on a plain notebook. Do this lots of times until you have a cute, spotty cover.

Draw a simple design on the front of your notebook in a thin layer of glue and then sprinkle it with glitter. Leave it to dry and then shake off any extra. Super-sparkly!

Why not see if you can do a design of Hello Kitty's face?

106

Turn the page for a sneak peek at

next adventure...

The School Trip

Tammy gasped as she slid across the ice rink with Hello Kitty holding one of her hands. Tammy hadn't skated before and was feeling wobbly. She turned the corner a little too fast and one of her skates slipped. She tumbled down on to the ice, pulling Hello Kitty with her.

They bumped down together and laughed. Falling over was just as much fun as skating!

Hello Kitty helped Tammy up and gave her a big

smile. The whole day had been fun from the moment she had chosen her outfit to go ice-skating in. Hello Kitty loved looking stylish. That day she had picked out a red skirt that swirled out when she spun round, a spotty top, thick tights, cream legwarmers and a matching cream scarf and gloves. She had finished the look off with a raspberry lip-balm called Raspberry Sparkle. Perfect!

Mama had taken Hello Kitty to the ice rink where Tammy and their two friends, Fifi and Dear Daniel, had been waiting. The four of them were great friends! They were such good friends they had even started their own club - The Friendship Club!

Hello Kitty smiled as she thought about it. The club had been her idea. They had membership cards and club meetings. They also organised trips like this one and had started to write a list of rules about friendship.

Hello Kitty held out her hand to Tammy so they could try again. They started skating around the rink once more but then spotted their friends, Fifi and Dear Daniel.

Fifi was a brilliant ice-skater and had skating lessons before school most days. Dear Daniel hadn't done much skating before but he was picking it up really quickly.

Tammy waved and Fifi and Dear Daniel skated over. He stopped with a swish of his skates and hardly even wobbled! Wow!

Hello Kitty was impressed.

Dear Daniel explained to Tammy and Hello Kitty that Fifi was a great teacher and had been helping him practice.

Fifi smiled and said that she'd happily show Tammy how to skate as well – amazing! Tammy thought that would be super, so off they went...

Find out what happens next in...

A HELLO KITTY STORY.

HELLO KITTY
and friends

The School Trip

Win Hello Kitty Goodies and prizes!

Collect the secret passwords in the first six Hello Kitty and Friends books, and go to **www.harpercollins.co.uk/HelloKittyandFriends** to download your exclusive Hello Kitty activities, games and fun!

Collect all six secret passwords to win super-special goodies!*

Coming soon: